Back to the Future

Author
Amelie Khare

Poet
Abigail Magaret

Art
Siddhant Shrivastava

Creative Director
Saurabh Shrivastava

Credits

© The Madhatter4children.co.in 2023

For any further information please address your emails to

themadhatter4children@gmail.com

Illustrations based on work of contributing artist - Siddhant Shrivastava and others artists & photographers of www.pixabay.com.

Lyrics and composition of Doryu song by Surfohif Pixabay

First Edition Print: September 2023

Book design, layout and setting by: Ess Designs - Pune

Contents

(Ray An's Poem written by Abigail Magaret)

Foreword

In the deep recesses of a child's mind resides the magical forests of imagination. I've heard the wellspring of fascinating stories spun from those dexterous minds; all of 5, 8, 9 ,12, 15 years and as they have grown enveloped a great scope and far reaching, more involved and almost eccentric wisdom.

I am always in awe of how they speak, question and carefully answer, thoughtful of the impression it creates on their own ability to express themselves. In fact, I learn from children how to grow in wisdom and understanding, to acquire and build upon. It isn't just another saying...child is the father of man... I would only add mother as well.

My life changed drastically upon the arrival of my first granddaughter, and grew exponentially with the second. I am old and grey but as the poet says , not with age but admiration of God's creation.

I pray to the heaven above that children resist the temptation of

metamorphosing into an adult creature. They suddenly become pithy , bland and self-centred, even suspicious. So, while the caterpillar becomes a chrysalis and then a beautiful butterfly, the same doesn't normally happen with the human race. If you are a child and you're reading this, learn. If you're an adult reading this – desperately unlearn. The lines of CSN&Y "Teach your children well, Their father's hell did slowly go by, And feed them on your dreams, The one they pick.... Don't you ever ask them, Why?" *

My granddaughters taught me the mistakes I made with my own sons. The greatest lesson I ever learnt from them is to be free, to think, to dream, to create and never matter if your dreams just blow away, that's one element of life you can re-create and live again, it doesn't matter how old or young you are. As a matter of fact, age doesn't matter - it's how you live your life inside of you. For what happens inside reflects on who you are on the outside.

Amelie was less than 10 years when she narrated this story to me in her nonchalant way, as if the imagery were everyday communication. The subtle yet determined words fell on my awestruck mind as I listened with bated breath. The story rolled off her tongue, as one of from the many well-worn books she reads to her little sister. It was there in her head waiting to be told, and I was the willing listener.

So read on, for on the pages between these covers, lies a world of dreams, of joy of sorrow, of happiness beyond measure. Live the dream and when it's gone wait there'll come another just as awesome, just as elating, just as sad and wonderful.

Just for today be a dreamer, one more time.
Cdr Maddox Hatter

** Lyrics Songwriters: Graham Nash*
  Teach Your Children lyrics © Nash Notes

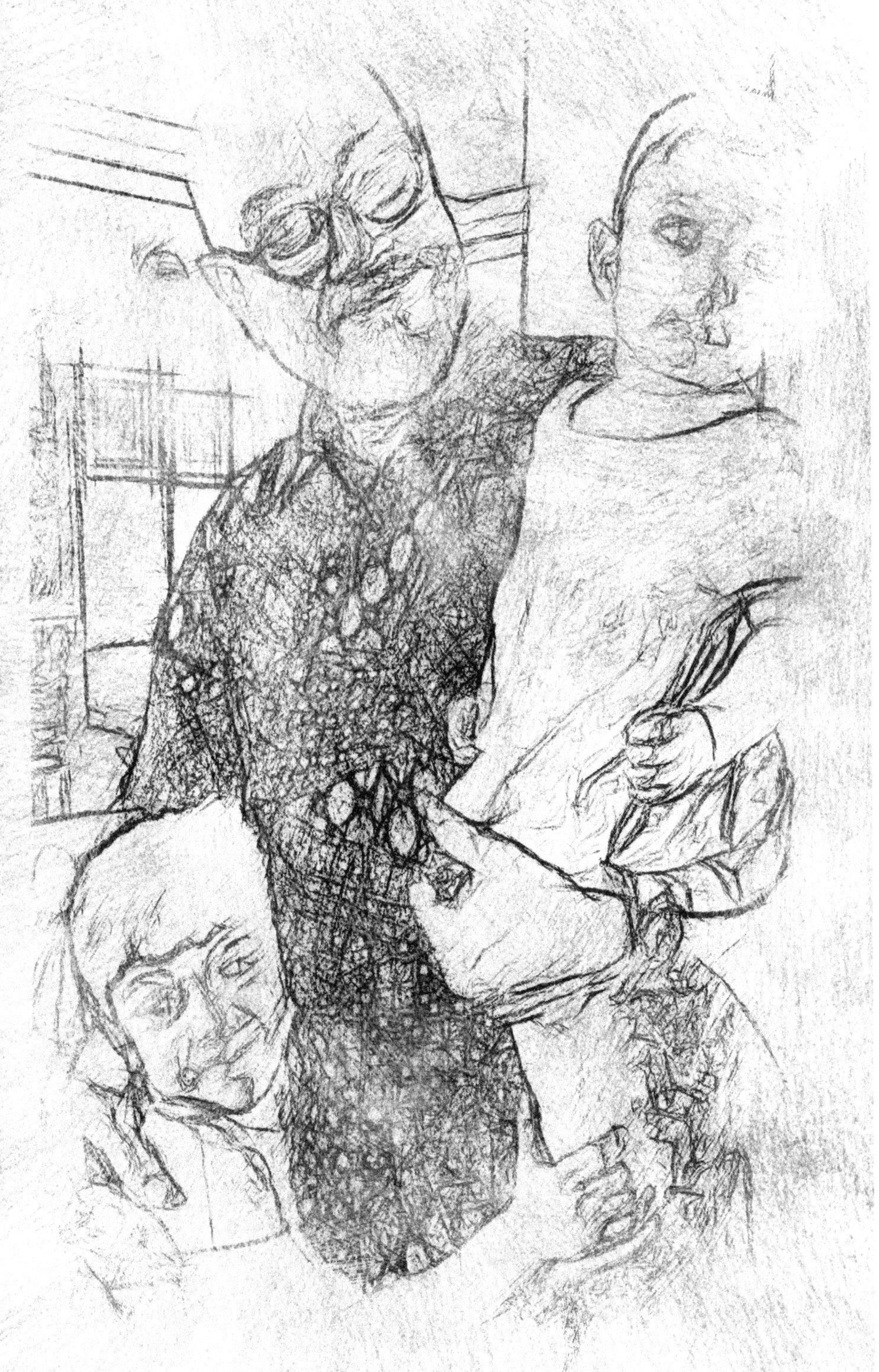

Doryu
Way of the dragon.

Drawn away from being the green twin of Earth, the blue planet, to the other side of the Milky Way, Doryu, is now nestled as the third planet to the twin star system of Regamedus. This solar system has nine planets only two are known to be inhabited. Doryu and the planet of Eibin. We all understand that gravity keeps a planet in orbit to a star. In such a stable environment it can work like a giant clockwork mechanism for billions of years. Great minds have been trying to work out the math of introducing a third object that skuttles the planet from its safe zone and flings it out to the frozen frontiers of Space. But to move a planet from one secure system to another, without loss of surface temperature, gravity, atmosphere and life....is an unbelievable feat of cosmic proportions. Well, that's exactly what happened to Doryu.

Eons ago, a tussle began between the creatures of Doryu and the Demon Dragon Emperor Belashahar's ancestor Wyvern . However, their hordes were unable to defeat and subdue the planet because, Earthlings intervened on behalf of the other Doryuan creatures, whenever the dragons seemed to be gaining the upper hand. Infuriated by their constant defeats, the Niddhoggian emperor devised a plan to have the planet dragged to the opposite side of the galaxy, without any creature ever feeling the shift.

The evil genius Wyvern

The evil genius Wyvern, had many a magic incantation that forced nature to be subservient to his command. Though quite honestly this was perhaps the most dramatic of all the spells he had conjured up and never been able to repeat. The only sign that something had happened was a flash in the sky. In that fraction of a moment Doryu was more than one hundred thousand Light years from its original position. A stunning feat of sorcery, even for the Emperor of them all. Whether the sheer energy in executing this task or something else, he was certainly weakened in strength and resolve. With every subsequent attempt to gain control of Doryu, the Niddhoggian grew weaker. In the current reign of King Bhimashtra of Pymra, the planet is firmly in the hands of the Pymrian Royals and the Queen of the Great seas. The king's sons Virann and Mihit An and the Queen Mother's daughters - Warrior princesses Amelika and Esmella, manage the day-to-day functioning, with advice from the Great Sage Grandriks who lives in the Castle of Phillislot, King Bhimashtra's abode.

Both the royal families of Doryu have had their share of misfortune at the hands of the Evil forces. The king of Pymra lost his wife in a surprise attack, when they were enjoying a day out in the deciduous Forests of the Northern Frontier. This devastating form of attack was fortunately never repeated, as it turned out to be too costly for the Niddhoggians. The Emperor of the Great Seas, Father of the Warrior Princesses Amelika, Esmella and husband of the Queen mother was also killed but that was in a skirmish. It was during the Allies confrontation with the dark forces early one evening in the winter of 9876, twenty years ago. There has not been a tragedy on that scale again. Many minor battles and skirmishes have taken place, either when the evil dragons are out kidnapping the young of other Doryuan dragons, in order to recruit them, eventually, or in turn when the Doryuan were raiding Evil dragon nests to rescue the young.

These continuous, though intermittent, battles have taken a severe toll on the numbers of Belashahar's force. The diminished count means he doesn't have the stomach to face the Allies in open conflict. So, there's the hit and run that has been adopted. However, these efforts appear to be few, far between and have diminishing returns, for the band of Evil outlaws, that this once awesome force has been reduced to.

Doryuans & their planet

The love and dedication towards the preservation of the planet is reflected in their efforts at protecting the diversity of all life forms. Every creature throws his or her weight behind the efforts to keep the planet free from pollution, garbage, of course no synthetic material is allowed to be used. All power is generated from water or the twin suns' rays. No fossil fuels are used, no trees are cut down; everything is recycled for further use. And if you ever happen to drop in on your way through the stars, it will do you good to remember this.

Metal for their weaponry is mined from the asteroid belt beyond the planets of the Regamedus solar system. It is hard work but they believe it's something they must do to preserve the planets' environment. They have the examples of Eiben and Earth. Those beings have ruined they planets by indiscriminate mining, logging, use of fossil fuel and consumption of synthetic material.

Every Doryuan is taught from an early age the importance of being clean, building green, recycling, eating mostly natural produce and being caring towards one another. Utopian lifestyle? Yes, one might say so, and they are actually living proof that it is possible. Remember, every natural ecosystem works in balance.

An ecosystem is a community made up of all endemic (flora &
fauna growing in the area) living things and the way they interact
with each other and the environment.

If any part of the ecosystem is damaged, it will affect all other parts of the system. For instance, if an animal goes instinct it could affect other plants and animals in the ecosystem, most of all if the animal happens to be on top of the food chain. But even a tiny insect like the bee is vital for pollination. Imagine, no bees no pollination results in no fruit!

Damage to habitats, like that caused by deforestation, can have a long-lasting effect, not just on the many species there, but also on the planet as a whole. Living trees help prevent climate change by removing carbon dioxide from the atmosphere and locking it away it in their wood, leaves and in the soil. Burning forests releases carbon, and removing trees increases the amount of CO2 left in the atmosphere, leading to global warming.

Trees and plants are also important for preventing the erosion of coastlines and for protecting against flooding, because their root systems hold the soil in place and they absorb excess water. Doryuans understand the importance and have very strict laws against anything that will pollute or damage the ecosystem.

Doryuan Landscape

The Doryuan landscape, for the most part, is composed of
relatively low-lying plains, plateaus, and older mountain
blocks. This dominates the younger, high ranges, such as the
Red and the Togan. The diversity of the land is breath taking.
There are four regions very distinguishable: the Plateaus,
ancient mountain ranges of Amberlain, towering above
the western plains; and the higher young Red and Togan
mountains in the North and Northeast, and of course the
fertile coast lands.

The Amberlain range hides the glacial areas that feed the
land with all the fresh water needs, without the creation of
dams and reservoirs. The resulting flowing streams are the
basis of the most fertile lowland soils. As the streams break
up into multiple brooks and even small rivers, they create
terraces, flat, raised surfaces alongside.

The physical structure of Doryu is dominated by a group of
ancient mountains of Amberlain run in a straight line and
break into two minor ranges as it runs closer to the western
shores of the giant mainland. This feature was formed more

than 350 million years ago, much like the topography of its sister planet Earth. The mountain ranges on Doryu mark boundaries where the planet's plates converge. Pieces of the crust are piled

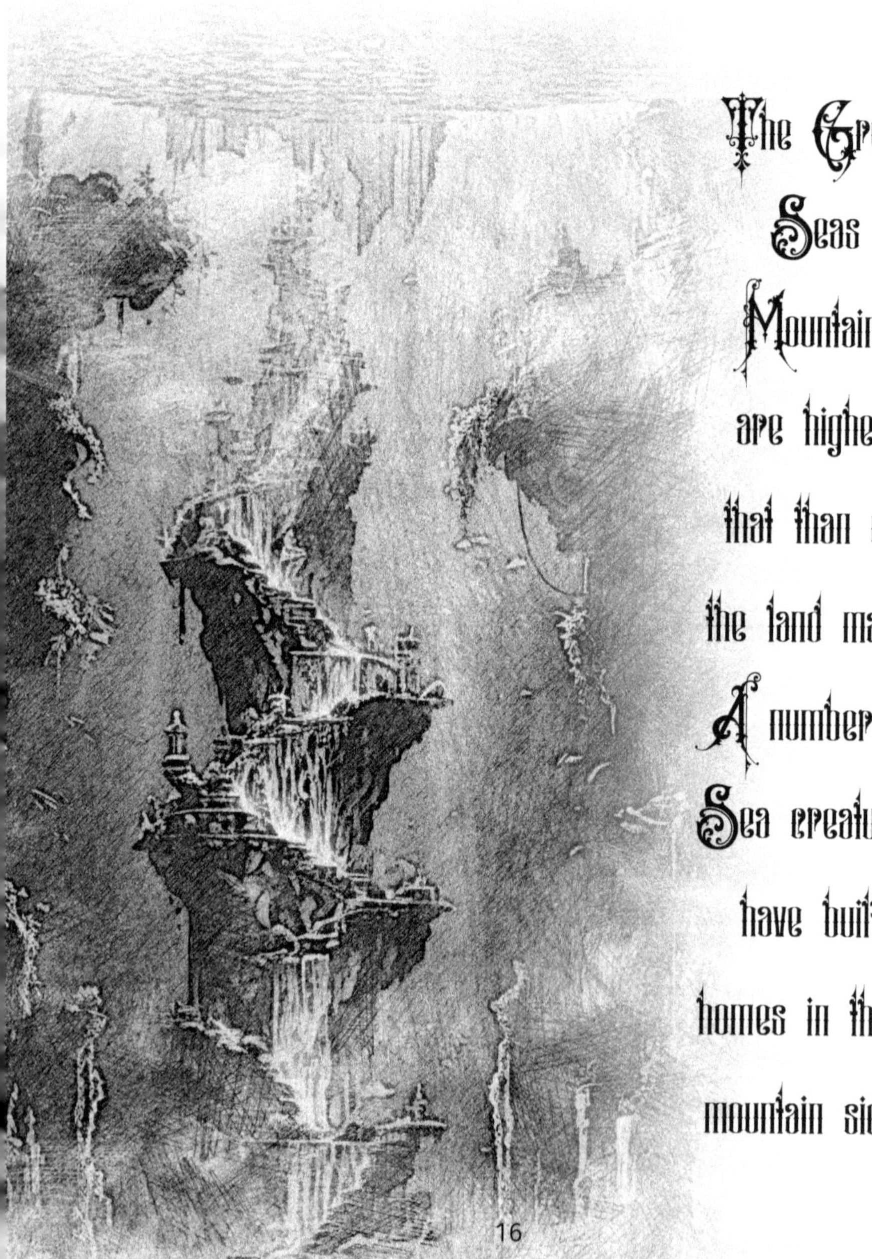

one on top of the another, creating complex patterns of folds and faults. Rocks deep within the mountains are re-crystallized into new mineral combinations as a result of intense heat and pressure.

As the mountains are pushed up, the soil erodes over time and these rocks are exposed. One can tell the histories of the mountains by the grains and colour of their rocks.

Earthlings recognise volcanoes as pockets where the earth releases basalt, a fluid lava from the mantle that erupts effusively and forms flows. Most earthlings' perception of volcanoes is that they produce dramatic, explosive eruptions. However, in the case of Doryu, the majority of the basaltic lava erupted along the Great Sea Mountains.

However, there are no longer any super explosions anywhere on Doryu. Nevertheless, the planet's core is still filled with molten lava. Although it is frequently referred to as the abode of the dragons, this is pure myth.

At "hot spots," where molten rock, or magma, develops in plumes of hot rock that ascend from deep below the Earth to pierce a moving plate above, there are very small eruptions. This is an extremely uncommon occurrence, though.

The Beings of Doryu

Doryu is an unusual planet in that it is inhabited by various species of beings. There are dragons of the flying variety, Fairies, Giants, Elves, Pixies, Human Barbarians and other forms of Homo sapiens, birds, animals, mythical beasts like Griffins and Hippogriffs, Gorgons, mammals from ancient earth, Dinosaurs, and a host of underwater life including mermaids and mermen. In ancient times there was a lot of travel between earth and Doryu and a lot of life moved from one to another planet, because of their proximity.

It's the reason you'll find prehistoric animals like Smilodons, Barbourofelis, mammoths and other extinct creatures still inhabiting Doryu, but not earth. This is primarily due to the conscious manner of the Doryuans action towards the health of their planet. While the predominant kingdom on land is ruled by Humans, the seas are ruled by mermen and mermaids, there are nonetheless a large number of Royal families who are heads of the species. Take Gaak of the Amphibians or Baron Von Algazia the dragon who took the form of a Human, and so on.

There were a number of humanoids sub species, even some with wings, similar to what Princess Esmella becomes when she emerges from the waters of the great seas.

Puffinadorhu, Philo & Grippin

The Warrior Amelika, as the Princess is preferred to be called, has a very special dragon for her ride. He goes by the name of Puff. However, his real name is Puffinadorhu (one born on Doryu), his parentage is not very clear however he belongs to the clan of the Klogins, the same clan as Belashahar the Evil King of the Dark forces.

At the moment the egg he was born from cracked open, the first light of the supernova Rhu struck him, light that took four billion years to reach Doryu, precisely on time and with such pin point precision, as to enter the opening shell of a baby dragon.

The effects were of enormous consequences for Puff, as he is fondly called, has magical colours that change with the angles of sunlight. More than that he is a specially pure creature deeply devoted to the protection of the Warrior Princess.

When the Princesses move about the land on foot Clawra and Storme, the barbourofelis and smilodon accompany them and of course Puff shadows their movement from the skies above. Because of his cosmic experience at birth, Puff's many character facets and abilities, keeps surfacing every time a situation arises. Like most dragons he has the powers to disappear and re-appear at will. He can communicate over long distances through special antennae which have grown on his head. He has an awe-inspiring wing speed of more than 80 beats per second that propels him to over Mach 3, if he so desires. In the Great Seas Puff transforms into a Peacock Mantis Shrimp the fastest and most brutal protector of the Princess.

Philo the hippogriff is the very unusual ride of Prince Virann, this legendary creature has the foreparts of a winged griffin and the body and hindquarters of a horse. Much akin to Philo is Chimera, the griffin and ride of young prince Mihit An. This mythical creature has the body of a lion, the wings and head of an eagle, a symbolical representation of the king of the jungle and the king of the skies with the ears of a horse.
Griffins are protectors from evil and witchcraft. They are courageous and very strong.

Doryuans are the most welcoming, friendly and amiable folk in the galaxy and beyond.

Keeper of the chronicles

Havamali is the ancient woman keeper of the chronicles of Doryu, no one really knew how old she is. She is assisted by her great granddaughter the most beautiful of the Valkyrien Maidens, her name was Frejyai. She is named after her famous ancestor Freyja. Frejyai did all the reading and recording of the events on Doryu, on a day-to-day basis.

Havamali depended on her great granddaughter, more than anyone in the family. The Valkyries possess some special powers. For instance, they can fly, by means of the so-called 'feather-cloaks'. They also have the to ability pass between planets, in any part of the Milky Way. They are custodians of the record of all the happenings of the worlds in the Universe. Every star system has a Chronicle keeper. It is the sacred duty of these creatures to maintain a record of all that happens on their respective planets, everything - the seen and the unseen events. Yes that's correct there are many things that happen, that we are unable to see with our eyes. Some folks however have a mind's eye!

Not all Valkyries are visible, most of them live life in the invisible form, appearing only when they desire to verbally communicate with other life form.

Niddhoggian Dragons.

Dragons have been a symbol of power and strength for centuries, revered in countless tales and legends. However, there is a lesser-known group of dragons: the Niddhoggian dragons. These dragons have long been known as the villains, responsible for the destruction of towns and cities, hoarding treasure and causing chaos and the eventual dislodging of Doryu from Earth's solar system. They are currently led by Belashahar who was the descendant of Nordicfafneer, the great Evil One of Yore. He was from the Klogin clan, not all Klogins were evil only the descendants of Nordicfafneer, they were called the Niddhoggians Klogins, to differentiate them from the others of the Klogin clan. Puff is the most prominent Klogin dragon who is not Evil.

Dragons per se

Dragons have long been misunderstood and unfairly maligned in popular culture. These magnificent creatures are often portrayed as nothing more than vicious fire-breathing beasts, intent on destruction and chaos. However, the reality is far more complex. In truth, Dragons are a complex and intelligent species, with a rich cultural history and a deeply ingrained sense of community. They are far from the mindless killing machines that

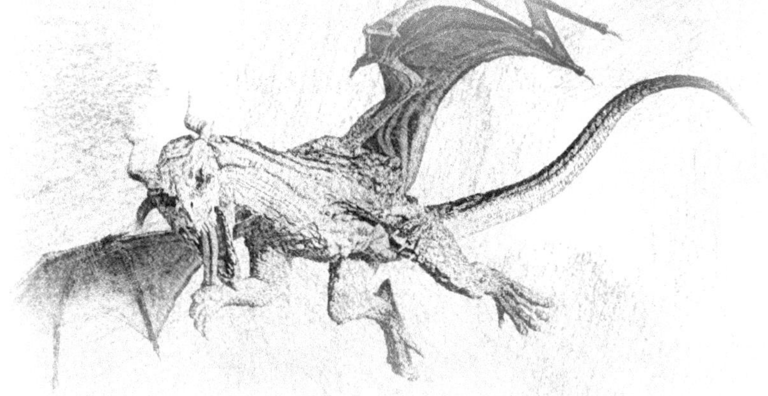

they are so often portrayed as. Only the Niddhoggian Dragons can be categorised as such. Dragons' reputation as fire-breathing monsters is particularly unfair, as it is based on a misunderstanding of their biology. Dragons do breathe fire, but only as a means of communication and defence. It is not an inherently violent act, but rather a way for them to signal their presence and protect themselves from perceived threats.

Furthermore, it should be noted that Dragons are not inherently aggressive creatures, Niddhoggian being the exception to the rule. They are only driven to violence when they feel threatened or when their community is under attack. In fact, they are known for their deep sense of loyalty and their willingness to protect their allies at all costs. Take Puff or Reese or Bholala, they are the classic Dragon examples. We should begin to appreciate the rich cultural history and complex social structures of these magnificent creatures.

Dragons are a rare creature that originate from the Nordic mythology. According to ancient legends, some dragons were known to dwell in the roots of the World Tree, Yggdrasil, and lived off of the corpses that would fall from the tree. This may seem like gruesome detail, but it speaks the cultural significance of Dragons in the Nordic mythology. They were also seen as protectors of the tree and its secrets.

Dragons possessed great wisdom and knowledge, as they were said to be the only beings aware of the true nature of the universe. For this reason, they were often sought out by royals and peasants alike for their guidance and advice.
Today, Dragons continue to hold great cultural significance. They

are no longer feared as harbingers of sorrow and misery and continue to captivate with their fierceness and mystery.

Their reputation has been severally tarnished by popular culture, which often portrays them as villains that hoard treasure and terrorize civilisation. It is essential to understand the impact of this representation on their survival and well-being. This is the primary reason why Dragons no longer exist on planet Earth. Dragons are not the only species that have been victims of this phenomenon. Many other mythical creatures have been misrepresented in popular culture, leading to negative perceptions and prejudices towards them. However, the problem with the dragons is that they are not fictional; they exist in the real world.

It is crucial to raise awareness about the plight of dragons and correct the misconceptions about them. They are not evil creatures; they are just different, with the exception of the Niddhoggians. They have unique abilities that are essential for the balance of the ecosystem, and they deserve to be respected and protected. By educating people about the true nature of these creatures, the folks of Pymra have not only co-existed, but ensured the revival of the dragon population on the planet Doryu.

Dragons are fascinating creatures that play an important role in the ecology of their habitat. These majestic creatures are known for their size, strength, and intelligence. They are found mostly in the mountainous regions of Doryu, where they coexist with other animals and plants in a delicate balance. Though now, a number of them have settled in the towns and villages across the planet. One of the greatest misconceptions about dragons, is regarding their feeding habits. It is often assumed that these dragons feed on human flesh and blood, but this couldn't be further from the truth. The exist on the same diet as the rest of the Doryuans, which is essentially omnivorous like most of the other inhabitants.

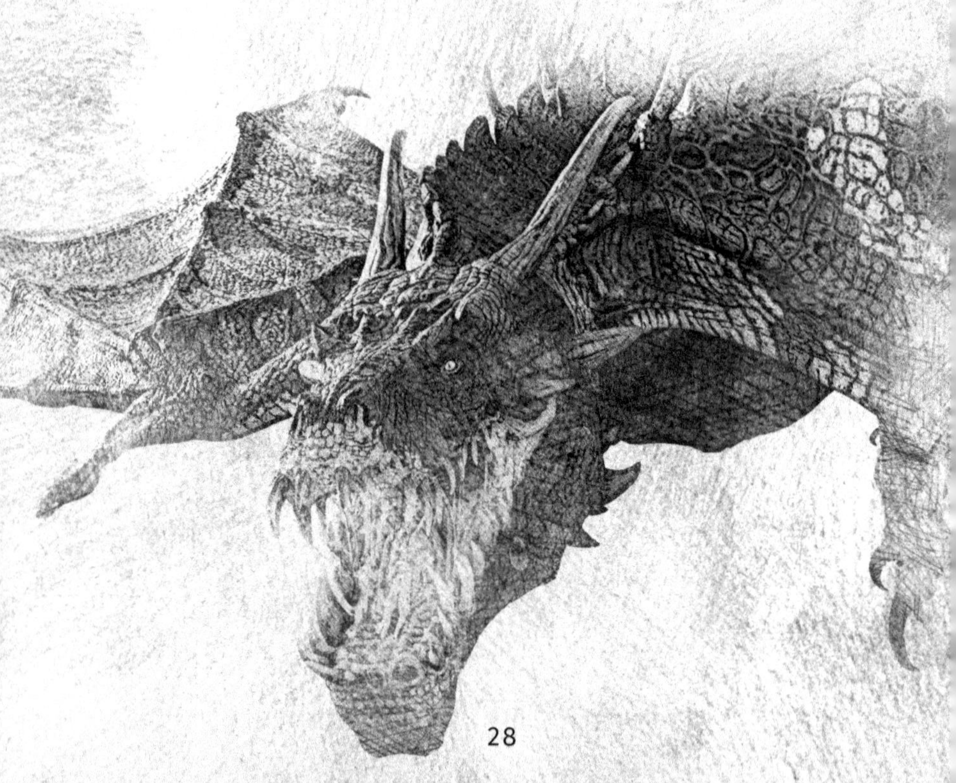

The Royal Families of Ooryu

The Great Seas:

The ocean has always fascinated us with its depths and mysteries. The world beneath the waves is full of life, from the tiniest creatures to the largest sea mammals. But what about the legends of mermaids and mermen? These mythical beings have been a part of folklore for centuries, captivating the imaginations of people around the universe.

The Royal Family of the Great Seas have ruled more than thousands of years, they are descendants of an earthling, the Macedonian, Alexander the Great's sister, Thessalonike. She was transformed into a mermaid upon her death in 295 BC (Earth age).

On earth, like elsewhere in the Milky Way, the world of mermaids and mermen has long been considered a captivating mystery. From ancient folklore to modern-day tales, these half-human, half-fish mythical creatures have been a subject of fascination. Whether they are portrayed as beautiful and alluring or as dangerous and malevolent, there is no denying that they have captured the imagination.

The Royal family of the Great Seas on Doryu rule over the underwater world with their magical powers and enchanting songs. Stories of their invincibility and charisma have been passed down through generations, with each culture having their own unique interpretations of these legendary rulers.

On planet earth, in some cultures, mermaids are depicted as protectors of the sea, helping sailors in distress or guiding them to safety. In others, they are seen as malicious creatures, luring sailors to their deaths with their sweet songs. Mermen, on the other hand, are often portrayed as fierce warriors or wise rulers of the underwater realm.

On planet Earth the history of mermaids and merman dates back to ancient times. The Greeks had their version of a mermaid

called "Siren," who was known to lure sailors with their singing voices, causing them to shipwreck. The Japanese culture also has a mermaid folklore called "Ningyo," which was believed to have a monkey's mouth and golden scales, and could bring storms and misfortune when captured. In West African mythology, Mami Wata, the mermaid is a water spirit. In Brazil, there is a legend of the Lara, a mermaid who lives in the Amazon River and lures men to their deaths.

Earth cultures believe mermaids and mermen to be water spirits who lived in the depths of the ocean and had supernatural powers. According to legend, they breathe underwater, swim at incredible speeds, and can communicate with all sea life. Mermaids and mermen are the descendants of a powerful and ancient sea god who reigned over the Great Seas for centuries, but our Royal family are descendants of Thessaloniki. They possess incredible powers, including the ability to control the tides.

The Royal family of the Great Seas, are revered by all sea creatures and the inhabitants of the lands of Doryu. They live in a magnificent underwater palace, adorned with precious jewels and shimmering with the light of a thousand bioluminescent creatures. Their power and influence extend beyond the sea, and that they have the ability to control the weather.

Mermaid and merman society is built upon a strict hierarchy, with each individual occupying a specific role. At the top of the hierarchy is the The Queen Mother, who rules over all the kingdom and also on the council for the Defence of Doryu (COTDOF). As the leader of Doryuan society, the queen along with other Royal Families is responsible for making decisions that affect the entire Planet .

The COTDOF is also responsible for ensuring that the society runs smoothly and that all members are taken care of. Below the mermaid queen are the mermaid princesses, Amelika and Esmella, who serve as her advisors and helpers. The elder Amelika is poised to take the throne and is therefore necessarily a brave warrior, acting on behalf of the Queen. They also serve as role models for the other mermaids and mermen and are expected to behave in a way that reflects the values and ideals of the society.

Beneath the mermaid princesses are the regular mermaids and mermen. These individuals occupy various roles within the society, such as hunters, gatherers, and caretakers. Each mermaid and merman is expected to contribute to the community in some way and to work together to ensure the welfare of their society.

The Kingdom of Pymra

The Current King Bhimashtra is a descendant of the ancient king Enmebaragesi of Sumer. The King of Sumer migrated to Doryu when the planet was near Earth and the Doryuans looked up to him to help them develop their society and to do battle with the Niddhoggian dragons, in order to keep control of their planet. Enmebaragesi often sort the help of his Earthling friends who obliged quite readily as they certainly didn't want evil dragons ruling the planet next door.

The Sumer kings were renowned for their learning and great administrative skills. The dynasty that ruled on Earth have left behind enormous records of their times. The archaeological discovery of the Sumer clay tablets sent shock waves through Earth world. They revealed in chronological order that this

ancient race learned and studied literature, made significant scientific discoveries in mathematics and the solar system. They obviously knew far more than the Greek philosophers, such as Plato (428-348 BC), and Aristotle (384– 322 BC) If we compare the Heliocentric System presented by Copernicus with the clay tablet drawings of the solar system we see similarities in the main core of the sun and the 5 orbits containing the planets around it. Extraordinary. Earth lost the great minds of the Sumers. Many of the other families of the followed their kings to Doryu as well.

Elves & Brownies

The Elves on Doryu are the descendants of Brownies the ancient industrious hobgoblins of the Scottish highlands. They were afraid of the human race and hence were rarely seen. Though they were heard at night pottering around the house cleaning things and settling the kitchen and doing other kinds of housework. When they eventually moved to Doryu, there was freedom. They feared no one and nothing, even the monstrous evil dragons. They were gifted known to communicate even with insects, sometime causing swarming bees to settle down quickly. The one love of their life was fine clothing! That still remains the most loved gift you can ever give an elf, especially the girls!

 Fairies

The word Fairy comes from various ethnics and languages. There is the word Fairy from Wild-Beast a Homeric name of the Centaurs, not true though. Or fée, the last syllable of nympha, or the Hebrew (peër), to adorn; Skinner, from the Anglo-Saxon word to fare, to go; others from Feres, companions, and even that Fairy-folk is quasi-Fair-folk. But the truest and most honest and correct answer is that the word Fairy is Celtic, from whom the fairies of the planet Doryu are descendants.

Faerie was the name of the place inhabited by Fays or Fairies and was set in the heartland of the Celtic world. These pygmy sized winged elves haunted the woods and dells of the hinterland of Anglesey where the blue druids actually danced to the shame of the invaders and protected the land.

They were eventually attacked and on the verge of annihilation, and so escaped to Doryu by crossing the Bifrost rainbow bridge at twilight. However, there were many migrations of Fairies from different parts of Europe, Africa and Asia over a period of time, when the pressures on human kind was felt by these intelligent and genteel creatures.

Be sure Fairies are not human but spirit that take the shape of humans to be seen by the world at large. However, over the eons of time, they are both comfortable and happy to be seen as such and have never reverted to spirit form. Though they may do so when threatened or need to escape captivity. On Doryu there is no such occasion to hide, so they are almost always visible to everyone.

The Great dynasty of Sages

Grandriks "Druid" sage, the word Druid is derived from the Irish word Doire which meant "oak tree" and signified the importance of nature. These Sages had a wide range of powers, and through their ability to contact other worlds were able to prescribe natural medicines and make crucial decision which always proved correct.

Though such sages were found all over the earth, from the British isles to all parts of Europe and Asia, however Anglesey was the most important location for their education from a common sage to a Druidi. It took more than 20 earth years to complete their education in order to become a fully-fledged Druid. There they would learn the intricacies of a complex lore which encompassed a broad array of topics such as ancient verse, natural philosophy, astronomy, the science of healing herbs and medicines as well as master advisors to the royal families everywhere.

Druidism was viewed as such a potentially dangerous vehicle of unity. This characteristic trait was demonstrated when the Druids fostered a united stand of all the beings of Doryu in wars against the Niddhoggian Dragons. They were fiercely loyal to the Monarchs of their lands. This loyalty was at the core of Grandriks character and actions on the planet Doryu.
Grandriks was of the lineage of King Arthur's right-hand man, Merlin who advised not only on all matters, including politics and war. Merlin also went by the Welsh name Myrddin Wyllt.

In closing

It will require an effort to chronicle the beginnings of all the beings on Doryu. That would take a humungous number of pages working within the confines of this book size. However, we will let you the reader discover the new and unique creatures, as each mysterious and wonderful adventure unfold on Doryu.

Back to the future

The happy ensemble of the strange ensemble ambled across the open fields toward the forest's edge, clapping to sound of Prince Mihit AN's and Princess Amelika's rendition of Doryu's favourite song.

I think I have the words,

I think I have the rhyme,

I try to play this verse,

I try to hold the time,

it's coming through my hands,

it's coming from my heart,

I don't know how it is

But here and now it starts

I play it out in the scented places

All alone I'm not that strong

A simple song from a simple man

I need someone to sing along

I am a lonesome player

Trying to get the message through

I just want to sing this song with you…

I didn't have a choice

Been quiet for so long

I knew I had a voice

But I didn't have a song

Something in me just cried out

But my words just slipped away

Then I heard you and your melody

And found the Words to sing

I am a lonely singer

trying to get a message through

I just want to sing this song with you

New Inhabitants from Earth

The song manifests just how much every living thing yearns the company of other beings, no matter the planet anywhere in the universe. It was such a finger-snapping tune that the creatures couldn't resist dancing as they moved along the path. Earlier that week Aarush, the elder of the Elf's Torp of Huldufolk, Village of the hidden folk, had officially invited the Royals to meet with the new settlers. These newcomers were from Rovaniemi, Finland a country on planet earth. They were from among the remnants who still resided on earth as the toy makers for the legendary old man called Santa Claus. He is that kind gentleman who sets out each year atop his fully laden, flying sledge to deliver the toys to poor children across the world.

These elves couldn't adjust to the rapid climate changes that were taking place on earth. It was becoming a lot warmer every year, but the weather was behaving more and more erratic and unpredictable. One day was warm, the next cold, the third day raining heavily! No one seemed to be able to forecast the weather anymore. The snow seemed to fall for a shorter period of time each year. Other elves and relatives from Earth had already moved to Doryu so it was the most logical choice.

The climate here is very stable, when it rains it rains, when it's time to snow, it snows. More importantly, Doryu was a spotless planet with no pollution and oh so very green!

The warrior Princess' sister Esmella, the prince's brother Virann, and the rest of the entourage, including Zerah the little butterfly fairy, Puff the magic dragon Amelika's ride (well, he flew overhead always watching out for the princess), Reese the shapeshifter, Clawra the barbourofelis, and Storme the Smilodon, also accompanied the royals. Their singing and laughter could be heard for a mile in front of them, so as soon as the forest edge came into view, residents of the elf village

heard the song and came out to cheer and welcome them.

Aarush stuck out his hand to greet the princes first and then the rest. The warm greetings exchanged and four new faces stepped forward. "May I present to you some of the newest citizens of Doryu… this is Dhanush, his son Ruhaan and twin daughters Ester and Ishya…"

"Hello, you beautiful girls", said the charming Princess Esmella. Amelika stretched out both her hands and took hold of one hand of each of the twins "My, my, two more red heads, how absolutely gorgeous!" she remarked with a warm smile spread across her oval face.

The Princesses then engaged the young red headed twins in a fun conversation. They talked about what the young girls would like to do now that they had decided to move to Doryu. "So, what do you girls like doing with your time?" asked Amelika "For me, a long stroll through the forest, calms my being so much. I just love the sound of birds' songs and see the various animals and hear their calls. Most of all I love trees…" replied an excited Ester. "For me it's the beautiful colour of the flowers and the leaves… I could spend a whole day just admiring the leaf veins and watch butterflies' flit from one flower to the other!" Ishya added.

"Oh, so you girls are the outdoorsy kind! Wonderful, the wilds of Doryu are the best place in the universe to explore for all its beautiful flora and fauna!" Esmella said, excited at the prospects of having new friends to show around.

"However, back on Earth we had little time for leisure, perhaps only in winter... but then the snow would cover everything like a blanket. We were so busy the rest of the year!" Ester said indicating, that we meant Ishya and herself, "Together we ran a successful business of making some beautiful knitted products. Our grandmother had taught us this trade. Of course, Elves are famous on earth for creating toys for children and home décor for the family." Ester declared rather proudly."
"Of course, all our products were made for Santa, so we really didn't have to go around trying to sell our stuff!" Ishya smiled.
"We were hoping to start it off here as well but we're not sure if it will work out (?)" Ester ending her sentence almost as a question.

"That will be a wonderful idea, am sure you'll get a lot of help from Aarush and the neighbouring village folk as well! In any case we have a village market day at Phillislot gardens every month end! Folks from all over Doryu bring their wares ... and most of it gets sold! – you're welcome there as well! said Amelika, happily.

"Wow! That's great!" said Ishya looking at a beaming Ester, "Thank you so much!" She said.

"Let me know if you need any help starting it up, I'll be very happy to introduce you to some relevant folk elsewhere as well." Esmella offered.

The men who were a standing a short distance away were discussing the weather, which was the staple conversation on Doryu. The Doryuans are very strict about keeping their planet free from pollution of any kind. So, a slight change in the weather or climate pattern, even an anomaly, quickly draws the attention of all the Doryuans. No synthetic material is allowed on the planet AT ALL, certainly no fossil fuel as most beings either had their own wings or used to ride on the backs of others who did.

But they had another important issue to discuss and that was the existence of the Evil Dragons. "Though I don't think you really need to worry about them, as they have eyes only for the capture or death of the Royals and their near and dear ones. They strongly believe that getting rid of us Royals will help them get control of the planet. They simply don't understand that it's the beings of Doryu, collectively, who detest their presence." Said Virann rather seriously.

"In any event at the moment they are on the back foot and mostly in hiding, in the red hills and forests of that area, some have been banished to the planet Iben, that's one of the outer planets of out dual star system." Mihit An added. "Oh, but I guess Bholala will love to fill you all in on our binary star system and everything that is Doryu" Virann laughed. Bholala was the principal of the Dragon school, he was a dragonet. A smaller form of a dragon, like a pony is to a horse.

 Ray An brings news of a dragon

While this discussion was on going, and as if to sully Mihit An's reassurance, a rather breathless Rayan the Giant stumbled out of nowhere and announced that an evil dragon had been captured not very far from where they were. "He was accosted by a patrolling party of warriors and arrested. He is being held there, in order to give you time reach there and question him" said Ray An addressing both the Princes and Princesses. All four of them take on a Hersir's role when needed. And you can bet they went into battle leading from the front, fearlessly. Noticing the new folks standing around, Ray An greeted them warmly, "Hello there, nothing that can't be handled I guess" he said his eyes darting back and forth between the red heads and the royals, not sure who he should be looking at.

"This, my new citizens, is the strongest being on Doryu! Rayan the giant! I am sure you'll meet him more often, seeing how excited he is to see you all!" Said Mihit An with a shadow of a smile on his face.

"We'll continue our chat once we check on who this nasty spike head is!" Amelika said in haste, "in the meanwhile let's not waste time, let's be on our way immediately" she said a fond goodbye to the twins. "Bethalaka!" the villagers shouted in unison. All of them flew off toward the direction indicated by Ray An.

Ray An, it must be said was a direct descendent of Rübezahl and his wife, the sister of Hlódyn, the mother of Thor. The family lived in the Forests of Bohemia, central Europe on the planet of Earth. It is said that they were the sons of the children of the Emperor who married earthlings. The few remaining evil giants earth were slayed, they included Goliath and his brothers.

Fafneer captured

As they landed they were confronted by a few of the Doryuan King's Guard, Warriors of the elite ranger Regiment. These battle-hardened chaps were afraid of nothing. In the midst was a frightened yet smarting young dragon anchored to a ball made of 1 gram of substance from a neutron star encased in Osmium, (there's nothing heavier than that in the entire universe). Doryuan's use it for captured Dragons, so even if they attempt a disappearing act, they will not get off the ground!

"Ok! yelled Ray An, "tell us what were you doing inside this cave?"

"I told you and am telling you one last time... I was trying to hide from these troopers, with a couple of other dragon friends. The others managed to escape but here I am, caught for inefficiently using my spirit powers of disappearing! My name is Fafneer, I swear am a new recruit, an escapee from Iben, I don't know the terrain very well..."

"Don't jerk us!!" Mihit An yelled. "Where were you going with the other dragons??"!!

"I don't know! We were told to meet Dynatroni the Niddhoggian recruiter, that sleaze-ball didn't turn up!!" The young dragon screamed back at the prince. Instantly one of the warrior's struck him with his Yllatri, (it's something like a taser ONLY much more painful).

"Okay, Okay," he flinched, "I did see strange things down there. People like you and this giant...though they wore some really strange clothes.... They sort of appeared and disappeared... I promise that's all. When we got out, I was captured by..." he said pointing in the direction of the warriors.

"Two of me? ..." Laughed a shocked Ray An "That must have been scary, eh?!"

"Ok, here's what we will do..." Amelika interjected to avoid them going off on a tangent. "You officers take this gent into custody and we'll return in the morning with some back-up and check out the cave system before coming to any conclusions."

Then she turned to Mihit An and the rest, "I think it's important that we have a conversation with the great Sage Grandriks, the King and General Uriah, before we think of any plan of action. We need to understand just what we might be getting ourselves into."

"In any case, please have the cave entrance properly secured tonight." Mihit An commanded the Warriors. "Maybe we should ensure this character is brought back here in the morning, when we arrive". Said Esmella matter of factly.

They all agreed with the arrangement and shot off towards Phillislot hoping to meet the Sage, King and the General as soon as possible. "Keep a close watch on the cave!' Virann shouted back to the sentries who had been posted there, though that command was quite unnecessary as these were elite troopers, the no nonsense types who take their duty to ridiculous levels of seriousness.

 Dawn, the next morning

At the break of dawn when shafts of light shot out across the assembly of strange looking warriors on their even stranger looking mounts. Not a very large group but ready in combat formation to fly out. So, they were waiting for the sound of the Rose Horn. These troops were instructed by General Uriah to accompany the Royals and their team in the search of the caves in the Red Hills near the northern frontier. He wanted to ensure there were no surprises with regards to the number or type of evil ones they could encounter. This was a result of the previous night's council meeting to discuss a plan to search the cave system where Fafneer was captured.

At the helm of the battle hardened force were the princes Mihit An, Virann and princesses Amelika and Esmella. accompanying the team was Zerah, Reese and a few others, after all they couldn't possibly miss out on this new adventure, now, could they?

At the sound of the Rose horn the dragons, hippogriffs, griffins and winged creatures lifted into the air in a silent but awesome sight. The suns' rays reflected off the bronze shields and body armour as the trees below bent their boughs to swirling wind force they generated.

They flew over the land as the suns' light penetrated the grey dawn, and when the smaller rays hit the dew-soaked fields, the sparkling gems of water droplets ricocheted bursts of shining light. Doryu landscape always appears breath-taking at this time of the day. However now, everyone's mind was focussed on what secrets the cave would unfold. There was really no time to enjoy the scenery. What a waste of a good moment, one would have imagined.

 The troop Hersir landed a few seconds before the royals. Mihit An, followed immediately. He dismounted and walked up to the dragon: "One last time I'm asking you; is there anything inside the tunnel that we should be prepared to fight against?" His voice broke the morning chill, in a crisp and menacing manner.

The Dragon knew this wasn't a time to play games. "I promise you, all that I told you yesterday, is true, nothing was false. If there are more of your kind there …I wouldn't know then, if you should be wary or not...how can I say?"

Amelika, who normally takes the lead in decision making addressed the group, "Alright listen up everyone... the Prince Mihit AN and I will lead a party of warriors into the tunnel...

princess Esmella, prince Virann and the others will stay here and stay alert ... If anything, other than any of us comes out of that tunnel..." she said pointing to the mouth of the Cave, "make sure you capture it or them. If you can't for some reason then destroy them. Is that clear?" she said looking each warrior in the eye, the words left her lips as each syllable was pronounced in a deliberate manner.

Entering the Mystery Cave

When she turned and with the prince entered the tunnel, the Hersir, his warriors, Ray An and Reese brought up the rear while Zerah flew above.... She had been extremely valuable in sneaking past the enemy unnoticed, when in difficult situations. They were cautious, and very tense ...the Hersir signaled to his warriors to stay together but walk in a line, across the width of the cave. This would ensure that every inch of the cave, from the entrance was covered.

However, very soon the narrow passage opened up into a large cave system ... they were confronted with a huge stalactite that had anchored into the ground from the high ceiling of the cave, creating a massive central pillar. They were standing in a giant hallway, from where several tunnels branched off in different directions.

"Hmm this is an awful predicament to be in. So, let's just stall the advance and think our next step through, carefully." Amelika advised. They stood still and quiet for a moment. The sounds of dripping water echoed and then there it was... faint sounds of what seemed like human voices murmuring ...

Zerah whispered, "I think I can hear some voices…should I go ahead and investigate…?"

The Hersir abruptly denied permission "No, I think it would be a good idea to stay together for the time being we shouldn't spread out as yet…"

There was an instant reaction from Mihit An "Silently…Quietly please … hand gestures and low whistles please, that only if you've something important to draw anyone's attention to."

They all crouched on their haunches but Amelika moved a few steps forward … suddenly she saw what looked like figures of humans but it flickered like a projection of sorts…on and off it went. She signaled to Mihit An with a low whistle and pointed up ahead…. They both went down on the haunches and stared ahead, to get a better view as they shaded their eyes with the palm of their hands.

Barely a few minutes later…the "vision" vanished altogether. The group split up, rounded the giant stalactite and joined up again, keeping a close formation as the Hersir had advised. They were still in the large cave hall, which extended before them for almost 100 feet or more, before the tunnels started in different directions.

Suddenly a stream of light burst through the rafters and shot out above them, it was almost like someone had turned on the lights of a dark room... Remember so far only the residue sunlight emanating from the cave entrance lit the area...and it was diminishing as they went deeper into the cave system. So, this burst of light startled the already tense group ... for a moment they remained stock still in an awkward crouched position. Soon they realised it was nothing to be concerned about, after all it was natural for sunlight to find its way through an opening in the cave, as the suns rose higher in the Doryuan sky. For a fraction of a moment, though, sweaty hands grasped their weapons even tighter.

Actually, the sun light was welcome since it lit up the cave and they could now see very clearly where they stepped. So, the pace of the progress further into the cave, improved. However, since dragons could camouflage themselves, it was still difficult to distinguish between the stalactite and the skin of a dragon, the lumps and bumps seems so similar. The only noticeable factor would be if a dragon moved, then they would become visible to the naked eye. Hence while they moved faster, it was imperative to keep their eyes pealed on every single formation ready for action in the event of a movement of any kind.

Remains of an ancient battle

The floor of the cave was strewn with broken rock and small stalagmites. As they moved forward very slowly and cautiously, one of the warriors pointed out the skeleton remains of a dragon, half protruding from the cave floor. However, the manner in which the skeleton was positioned, one could conclude that this dragon died in a fight. Though nothing suggested that was a recent event. There had been so many skirmishes and it wasn't surprising to find something like this on the floor.

The keeper of the Chronicles, Havamali had mentioned the many battles with the dragons and how they had retreated into the myriad caves of these hills and mountains. So, it wasn't unusual at all to find such skeletons. Amelika nodded in acknowledgement and waved for the team to continue their cautious journey into the cave, one step at a time.

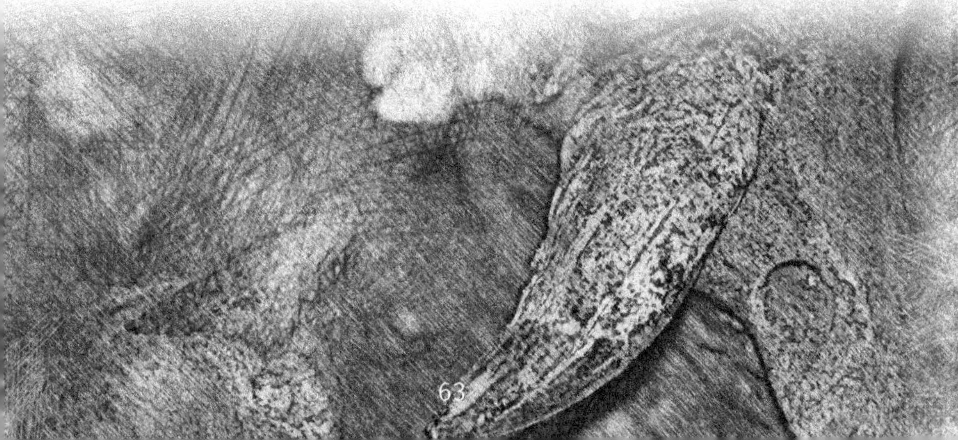

Voices in the dark

It was then they experienced the strangest thing on Doryu yet! They heard voices, that seem to come from somewhere very close ahead of them,

"Who are these? look like some of our own, but I don't recognise any of them" said a voice that sounded very commanding. Immediately Mihit An shouted out into the empty space before them, "Who goes there?!"

There was a moment's silence… now everyone was on high alert and very tense, expecting a battle to commence any moment… naturally they froze in their tracks… eyes darting across the cave in front of them to try and figure out what it was…

"I can see you…friend …why can't you see me?" Came the reply from the unseen source. Every member discretely tried locating a hiding spot in crevices or behind rocks. Some even lay down behind the protruding stalagmites, in order to take cover and waited.

"Who are you …. where are you… we can't see anyone? If you are not with the Evil dragons, you have nothing to fear… show yourself…" Mihit An said sounding more reconciliatory this time.

"What do you mean you can't see us? We are here, right in front of you, all 20 of us and you can't see us? That's difficult to

understand," said the voice. "ok can you see this." Suddenly a small rock hit the ground and kicked up dust, just before Mihit An, but it seemed to have come out of nowhere! It made the warriors crouch even lower, if possible, awaiting orders on their next move.

But Amelika was aggressive as she stood up and shouted, "Are you with the forces of the Evil ones or on the side of the people of Doryu? Answer!"

This did not appear to rattle the strange voice, who shot back "You speak like a princess, I am the king of Pymra, and these with me, are my loyal subjects."

"Father? That can't be you, we left you at Phillislot, sitting in the command control room with the general and the great sage. Who are you why can't we see you?" now the tone of his voice softened as he stood up and took a step forward.

"Don't make a joke of it …my son was slain by that devil Tantara leader of the dark forces… so how can you be my son? Is this another trick of that hideous creature of a dragon? who are you?" the voice sounded very agitated, almost angry.

"Now who is this Tantara? And it sounds like he is ruling the evil ones." Said a very confused Amelika, she spoke almost to herself. "Could this be an illusion? Something that is yet to happen in time and… it could be that we have hit a time warp?"

"That could be the answer! We know Belashahar's son's name,

never heard of Tantara?" Ray An mumbled.

This encounter was getting stranger by the minute and it unnerved the Doryuans, it was one thing fighting an enemy you can see, even a fierce one; but when you can't see and don't know what you are up against, it sends a chill down the spine. However, Mihit An was still mulling the Voice's response about his son "Why do you say that, if you are the King of Pymra then I am your son…I am here in flesh and blood!"
"It can't be, firstly I know my son is dead and, in any case, you don't look like my son… especially with those ancient clothes you're wearing?" The Voice appeared to be equally confused. Hearing what the voice said, Ray An turned to the Princess and said rather urgently, "I think it's time we got Grandriks here as soon as possible."

Urgent need for Granriks

Amelika nodded in agreement, "I agree, Zerah you fly with Puffe and bring Grandriks here immediately. Don't waste time doing anything else, and please don't end up having a long conversation with Tini, Gaak's sidekick, I'm sure that nosey-parker, will ask you why you are rushing around?"
Zerah slipped back out of the cave and signaled to Puff to follow her. She startled Esmella and the other warriors, but she didn't stop to explain anything.

"Sorry, but please be on alert!" she pleaded with Esmella, "We're going to Phillislot to carry Grandriks back here...that's all I have time to say just now..." Esmella ordered the warriors to take up commanding positions in front of the Cave and instructed that Fafneer be taken out of sight. It didn't take very long for her ordered to be actioned.

Back inside the cave, Amelika encouraged Mihit An to engage the Voice in conversation for as long as it took Grandriks to get there. "Your Highness how exactly did Tantara end up defeating the mighty forces of the Royal Families of Doryu?"
"Well, it wasn't an all-out battle, at first. For many years they

showed themselves in numbers at the edge of the territories, but would soon disappear… they never harmed anyone. As much as we could, we responded to the calls from concerned folks, but since the evil ones never really did any harm, our reactions were slowed over a period of time. I really don't think we understood theirs was a change in strategy. Eventually the citizens got tired of reporting their presence and got used to seeing them around…." And the long saga unwound itself as the king explained in great detail the cunning and ferocity of the evil dragon King Tantara and his forces.

Slowly the picture emerged of Tantara as a ruthless and shrewd leader… but the discourse was interrupted by the arrival of Puff and Grandriks. It was within the hour that the great sage was standing right beside the Doryuans, facing the voice.

At the sudden appearance of Grandriks, there seemed to be a lot of commotion in the invisible world in front of them. Many a gasp rent the air as the Voice spoke again "Great sage of Old is it you sage Melinix, my lord is that really you?! We've searched for you across the glens, mountains in the east and down into the depths of the oceans … we didn't find you anywhere!"

It took no guessing, Grandriks signaled that he knew exactly what they had encountered, but first he had to reassure the aggrieving voice. So, in his wise way Grandriks explained to the Voice not to worry that they would find a way to rescue them, but first since they could not see who was speaking to them, Grandriks asked, "Sir what is your good name?"

"I am the grandson of the Great King Bhimashtra, and the Son of King Virann, my name is Bhimsenna I am the king of Pymra." Said the voice that appeared regal yet in mourning.

Mihit An and Amelika, almost let out a cry in unison! What? Prince Virann's son. Virann wasn't even betrothed as yet. Who would he marry? All sorts of questions flooded their heads. Grandriks smiled and raised a hand as if to reassure them. Thank goodness they had brought the Sage here, or else they wouldn't know how to handle such a strange and awkward situation. But they trusted Grandriks implicitly, he knew how to manoeuvre the conversation and bring the situation under control.

Amelika had always been entrusted for her intelligence and leadership skills. In fact, her quiet and confident demeanour made her the obvious choice for most negotiations, which she either led or was the main spokesperson. This was the first time outside of the palaces that someone else was actually involved, besides herself.

Bhimsenna explains

"I now understand your highness! Do explain to us how your highness and his loyal followers are stuck here in this tunnel; are you in a tunnel or are we just seeing an illusion?" Grandriks enquired, his deep soothing and gentle voice seemed to bring a sense of calm among both the seen and the unseen forces that faced each other.

"We are in a tunnel, indeed and are hiding from the Niddhoggians dragons led by Tantara. He is the grandson of Belashahar, whom the great King Bhimashtra, my father and the royal families defeated and sent into hiding! I understand that my grandfather and my father decimated the dragons and banished many to Iben. If the chronicles be right, my Lord, Tantara was born in your days on the isle of Vimandara. We learnt that He was raised there in secret and sent to the planet Darius by some of Belashahar's loyal hordes to learn the art of warfare." Said the Voice, now in a calm and collected tone.

"Darius? We didn't even know if anything existed on that planet!" gasped Reese. "There's so much happening that we are simply unaware of!" Zerah agreed. An equally shocked Amelika couldn't help interjecting…without sounding rude, "My Lord, you know how fervently we have searched for the Niddhoggians' nest to rescue eggs and babes that they dragonapped from the other loyal dragnitizens of Doryu. My lord, when they are rescued we bring them up in our ways, so turn them from Evil habits and make good dragnitizens of them… It has been our belief that we have been very successful in doing so… obviously something is amiss!" she said looking toward Grandriks.

"But how is it you didn't get Tantara… or else we wouldn't be in this situation now, would we?" Remarked the voice, the gravity of his voice echoed in the cave and silenced the entire company. Yes that's unfortunately true, the Doryuans would have to double their effort and expand their operations to include all planets of their solar system. The political and security position on Doryu was at a crucial juncture in their historic and epic war with the Evil Dragons, and the Doryuans were simply unaware of the growing possibility of an impending doom.

The Doryuan's were shocked into silence for a minute. The air was thick with anticipation and especially Amelika could almost feel the weight of responsibility upon her young shoulders. "What are we doing? Why are we so blinded? Why can't we see that the diminishing encounters with the Evil ones, can only mean they are up to some no good!" she rebuked herself, under the breath.

It was Grandriks who broke the weighty silence with an urgent call to action.

"There's no time to lose. We can change the course of history if we act now!" Looking at Amelika, who was undoubtedly in a daze, he said "Take a crack team of warriors with you and rush to the isle of Vimandara… search every crevice, canyon, hill and glen in those mountains and plains, high and low… you just must find the baby Tantara don't stop, it must be a round the clock 24 X7 continuous task, till you find Tantara. Please involve the Baron von Algazia after all it's his domain, and remember if he is such a valuable asset, then he is bound to be well guarded… While Belashahar may not be there, himself, I am certain he will have his best of those maggots around. So, take full precautions, take a larger force if necessary, attack from many sides … don't let them notice a large single contingent coming toward them… there must be an element of surprise. Capture him if you can and take him back to Phillislot… guard him with the best of warriors and let Bholala teach him the ways of all things good, the way of the beings of Doryu. If you can't don't leave him alive, remember it's not a hatchling that you are slaying but the possible mass murderer of Doryuans, the apocalypse that we all hope will never come. I won't leave the cave but will remain here with His Highness King Bhimsenna, now there's no time to waste… hurry!"

The search party heads out

With that Amelika and Mihit An reacted instantly. Mihit An instructed the Hersir to select 3 of the best warriors to remain behind in order to guard the Sage and the unseen forces, if they only could, against any possible attack. Having thus supposedly secured the cave, he along with Amelika and the rest of the warriors hurried out of the cave as silently as they possibly could.

They left behind the Hersir and 3 battle hardened warriors with Grandriks. Grandriks settled in for a long wait as he rested his back on the tall stalactite with the sentries surrounding him, looking outward. As they were reaching the mouth of the cave they could hear Esmella scream out an alert command. When the eventually surfaced they found themselves surrounded by Esmella and the rest of the warriors.. and a startled Fafneer stared in amazement at the precision stance taken by the small disciplined force at the entrance to the cave. "no wonder the unruly Niddhoggians find it hard to defeat these well-trained valiant fighters."

He thought to himself, "what a fool I have been, I should have taken the advice of Dilong the hornless one, I should have defected when I could have." He sighed and rested his head between his front feet and dreamed of better days.

There was a distinct urgency and clarity in Amelika's quick instructs, she related the happening in a nut shell and then.. "Esmella follow us with your group. But keep a distance between us so as not to appear we're all together.." Esmella knew exactly what her sister wanted. Virann and Esmella led the group which travelled several kilometres to the left of the main party.

It was difficult for anyone to assume these were on the same mission. In the meantime. Amelika had instructed Reese to inform General Uriah of the urgent need to have two groups of warriors of a larger strength approach the isle from the south and south west at warp speed. One of the forces should be led by Baron Von Algazia and the other by either Major Mordecai or Samudra.

Esmella had a hard time digesting the fact that they had just left behind Virann's son in the Cave!! "What did he look like, who did Virann wed and ...oh there was too much to unravel ... now she needed to focus on the mission ahead.

Virann is angry

" No one is going to believe this when I tell them!! Especially mother! My goodness! But let's fly we must keep pace with Amelika and Mihit An's team!" She yelled out to Virann. Virann was just flying blindly his thoughts were a whirlwind, he just couldn't come to terms with the fact that his son the future king was in danger of dying and with him with the entire legacy of Pymra would be lost.

"My son ! Mine!" he said to himself again and again. The precarious nature of his family dynasty's future, began to have an impact on his nerves. " Got to keep my wits about me, got to lead from the front, to act wise, fight hard … " he kept repeating these inane words to himself again and again. He couldn't put it out of his mind.

Amelika said "Come on puff we've got to get there as quickly as we can!" She explained to Puff about Tantara and how he could be a baby in hiding, the grandson of Belashahar. If they could find him and bring him back to Bholala to make a good Dragon out of him… "then the kingdoms on Doryu would be saved from future destruction." She said.

"I'm so anxious … we must try to locate Tantara, capture and take him to Bholala. For once I don't have the stomach for the idea of killing a dragon hatchling, evil or not." That was very unusual for her to remark, though Esmella was the more sensitive of the two sisters both were tough warriors. "Come to think of it that's something I have never had to do…so far at least…yes I was involved in the battle against Karantika and sadly slew her but never a young hatchling…so I sincerely hope we don't have to do that now….!"

Virann was a little upset with her kind of reasoning, "You're talking about the potential killer of our families and my son! I really don't care - if he's still in an egg or just born or an older hatchling … no question I'd kill him on sight, if I have to, without a pinch of remorse. I strongly recommend that you do away with your misplaced ethics, this is not an issue of some barbaric infanticide. You can have my word for it you will have to encounter many a brave, strong and vicious Niddhoggian guards who will certainly be around that little devil. They won't think twice of slaying you or any of our young or old. To them he is the future, after all he is royalty, isn't he?"

The objective in sight

The scout in the lead signalled with his raised hand, that the Isle was sighted just ahead. Amelika immediately signalled as well, using hand motions to tell everyone to gently descend to a lower altitude. Putting a finger to her lips she commanded that everyone keep complete silence from here on.

Amelika's was the first team to reach tree top height, while the squad led by Virann and Esmella followed many kilometres to their left. And across the water, two groups of warriors could be seen soaring toward the island's beachead from the mainland, practically skimming the waves of the emerald seas. It would be difficult for anyone observing from the island below to tell the warriors that were skimming inches above them from the foam spray on top of the waves.

They then landed in the jungle at the foothills of the island's center after flying low over the sands. All of the groups descended in different places, nearly encircling the island on all four sides. As they moved further inland the search began in earnest. Reese was sent out to scout the area in an effort to be as quiet and covert as possible. Because of her flawless shapeshifting abilities, she could even transform into a rock or a tree. She was delightfully deceiving and did well in such circumstances.

Each group commander indicated to their warriors to spread out in a straight line in order that they search the area with a fine-tooth comb. Despite the great number of them, they couldn't be heard as they progressed through the jungle floor, searching behind every rock, up every tree and in every hole in the ground. It was half way through the jungle and they had reached the foot of the mountains when they realised nothing had shown up yet. They had combed the entire forest belt around the mountain but found no sign of Evil dragons or their nests.

The progress slowed to a snail's pace as they began their ascent of the mountain side. One of the warriors raised a hand and everyone stopped in their tracks. Up ahead the could hear a grunt and the brushes rustled as if something was scurrying along in the undergrowth... a warrior dashed ahead with great speed to encounter the mysterious sound... but out came a startled wild boar ... it looked at the warrior and then turned around and hurried back into the undergrowth as fast as it could... He turned around with a sheepish smile on his face. All that running through the brush made a lot of noise. If there were any Niddhoggians, they would certainly have been alerted by now.

However, they hadn't gone a few hundred feet when ...they encountered the entrance to a large hole in the mountain side! They are fell silent and stood motionless, signally that they should wait till the Mihit An inspected the way ahead...he creeped all the way up, almost crawling on all fours and peeped into what appeared a dark hole!

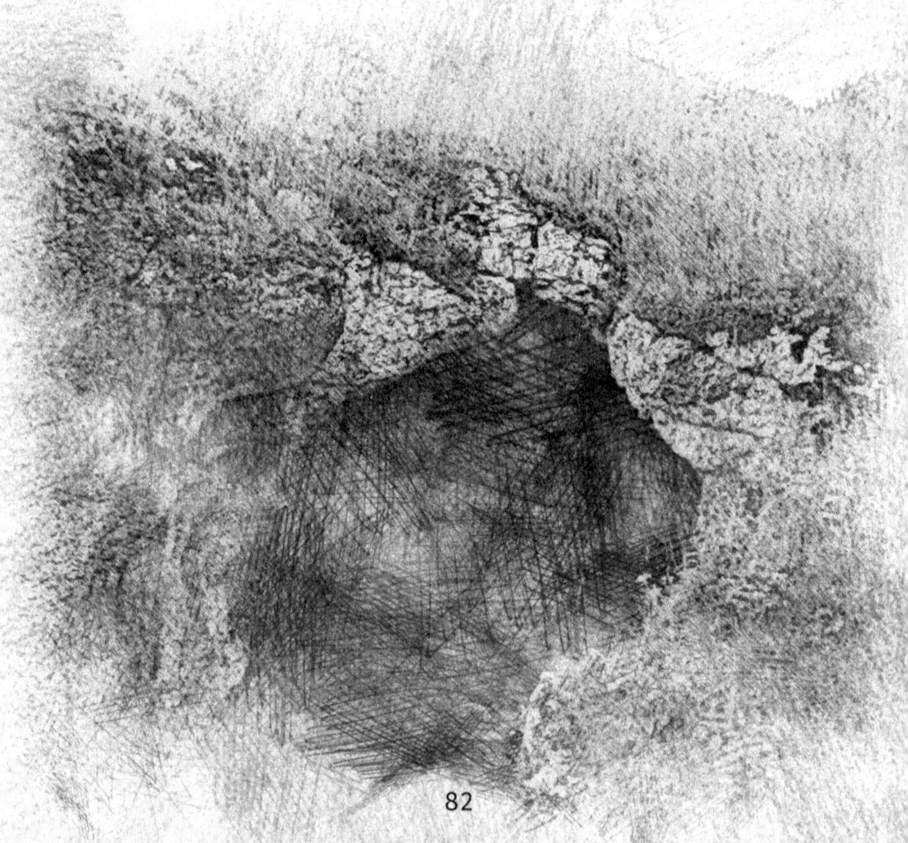

Surrounding the mountain

Amelika whispered instructions to Ray An, "You and two warriors circle around to the other side of the mountain and search for any exit that may exist there … just in case we do encounter dragons and they attempt to flee through the back door. We shouldn't take any chances with these crafty devils!" Ray An: "will do, come on guys let's head up and over the shoulder of the mountain, quick!"

Finally, Mihit An gave the all clear and Virann, and the princesses entered the cave. Almost immediately they could hear soft strains of music…strange they thought… and then waved to the rest to follow into the cave… moving carefully deeper, they found themselves in the middle of a huge hall in the middle of which was a siren playing and singing…

Esmella shouted urgently, in a restrained manner though, afraid that she would be heard by the Evil ones "Quick turn your eyes aways from her, don't look at her or focus on the music… I know this one very well, it is Jezebel the evil gorgon… she has transformed into a siren… she is probably sent to lure anyone away from finding the hatchling Tantara...So we are on the right track!"

Everyone focussed their minds on looking for the baby dragon and shut out the music of the siren from their minds... This quick reaction saved them from, almost certain, disaster.

This was only the first of many more illusions they would have to avoid while moving ahead...in the next open area they found a strange looking king sitting on a throne carved from the cave rock itself... only this time they were more prepared to ignore the illusion and so they continued their careful trek further into the cave system... all the same they manoeuvred cautiously as they worked they way around the image of the king...just in case there was any real trouble... when they turned the corner into the next room they came upon a wall...a dead end, it seemed they could go no further... the wall had a mark of a dragon on it...

Mihit An: Now what?

Esmella: "It's probably an illusion also, but let's be cautions, what we do now could warn the Evil ones of our impending approach."

Amelika: "what do you mean? Zerah go ahead and investigate, see if you can fly through the wall...."

Zerah was a brave little fairy, and without another thought flew straight at the wall .... "Okay wall let's see if you are really rock!"

she said with a determined look on her face.

The moment Zerah's hand touched the wall it disappeared and
another great hall came into view...

"Just as I thought" said Amelika, "Now we have certainly set
off an alarm of some sort so I think we ought to be VERY VERY
careful from here on."

The battle begins

No sooner had the words left her lips when suddenly a large image of a Dragon came into view… it seemed like a statue (?)… Mihit An looking at the eyes of the dragon, called out a warning "Cautious everyone…warriors draw your weapons and point directly at the head of the Dragon please! Hold the target while you continue to advance forward". There was a sense of urgency in his voice.

When they got within shooting range…suddenly the statue let out a spine-chilling roar… and it opened its mouth to let out a stream of almost blue hot fire…
Mihit An screamed out his order "Shoot now everyone! Now!" The jet flame throwers of the warriors blazed directly at the Dragon's head even before the blue flame could cause any damage! With a loud scream he crashed to the ground in burning embers… that scattered the team. Now they were all exposed right in the middle of a cave hall.

Amelika shouted "get behind a rock or any other object you can put your body behind, now! Quickly!"
There wasn't time enough though, because seconds later they

came under attack from two sides. So, before you knew it …
they were in the middle of a fierce battle that raged on inside
the cave system…The warriors were as determined as ever so
they pressed hard to keep moving, encouraged by Amelika and
Mihit AN. This wasn't a battle of do or die, this, after all was a
matter of the future of their planet and every Doryuan, who at
this time had no clue to the danger they were in. There were
loud screams, roars and sounds of fires streaming from the open
mouth of dragons.

The dragons didn't have the luxury of turning invisible to hide
as the special Doryuan flame thrower guns illuminated them! So,
they were forced to stand and fight. For a while they seem to be
holding their positions, despite the fierceness of the warriors'
assault who were egged on by the words of the great sage
Grandriks

 "You'll do well to fight for life and home, for what lies before
you is the beautiful dawn of another Doryuan day of freedom!
Freedom, the very breath you take must cry out though your
muscles burn in pain, fight on brave warrior, fight on – 'tis not
just you but for all you love, fight on! Let your battle cry ring
out across the land and let your enemies tremble at the sound
of your footsteps. Victory is within your grasp, so fight on, you
brave warrior, fight on!"

Eventually one of the dragons, who couldn't take the pressure anymore turned to flee while the other was slain... the warriors were tensed waiting for yet another onslaught, a few minutes later...nothing... so they cautiously advanced into the next cave area all the while listening and waiting for a possible surprise attack. The progress was slow but very cautious. Another flash of light and the warrior to the left of Esmella was hit.

Mihit An shouted: "down everyone" ...
Amelika: "There he is ...above the green over hanging rock ... and she fired with her flame thrower hitting the dragon in the belly and he came hurling to the ground, with an ear-piercing roar... he was writhing in pain so the hessir put him out of his misery with a blast from his powerful ray gun.

The begining of the end

The advance commenced once again … there appeared to be an opening at the other end of the cave as light streamed through and this time, they could hear Ray An the giant shout loudly: "And where do you think you're going young lady? !"
Then a crash of fire and blood curdling scream of a dragon…
 "Got him oh eh her" Ray An cried out in triumph…. "This must be the young Tantara…"

Amelika and Esmella rushed out of the cave …shouting "Wait! Wait!" …as Ray An was about the finish off the drakaina. As they reached her side, she had one hand stretched out to cover a baby dragon that was curled up beside her and the other preventing Ray An from firing his jet flame gun!
What they saw shocked them and they sank to their knees beside the mortally wounded Dragoness.

"Don't hurt him please he is my son…. I am not an evil dragon but was stolen from my mother's nest many years ago… this my son Tantara, he's too small to know anything about the wickedness of these Evil terrors… I have tried many a time to escape the wickedness of these monsters and in an effort to come to you, princess Amelika... I knew you would understand, that you would help me... but I could never... when I was forced to wed the wicked king of demons, I swore I would do all in my power to make sure my children, if I ever had any, would not meet with the same fate... I was ready to pay with my life and so destiny quickly obliged...

I came out of the cave because I knew it was the chance of a lifetime to escape with my son... but I didn't know the Giant wouldn't know I was not one of these hideous monsters..." her voice was shaky and she struggled to speak... "before I could say anything he fired... no I cannot blame him... so now please take Tantara and bring him up in your care, I beg you"... tears mixed with blood rolled down her battered face... "do not to allow him to be taken..." mid-sentence she passed away, her eyes were open and looking straight at Ray An the Giant, who by now was also kneeling down beside her lifeless body.

Esmella moved closer and rested a reassuring arm upon his giant hand, "How were you to know she was a good being? – remember it's not who we war against but with what we war against – the evil that they represent. I often imagine if all the evil dragons bear an evil heart? or are they trapped by the Beelzebub, the lord of the flies and all things filthy and evil?!"

Ray An, the powerful one, was so overwhelmed with emotion that he was brought to tears. He knew his grave error of shooting first and talking after. That's because they could neverb trust evil dragons, it was always kill or be killed. Every Doryuan was trigger happy on encountering an Evil Dragon. And in this particular instance there was really a chance of being killed, because he couldn't have known that this drakaina was the only good thing to emerge from the darkness of this cave.

Just then the princes and the other warriors emerged from the side of the mountain and saw Ray An and the others standing over a dead dragon... The princes were surprised by the sombre gathering that greeted them when they emerged from the cave... they had no idea what had happened a few minutes before. Inside the cave they were busy mopping up any resistance that may have come from the one dragon that purportedly fled...he didn't actually, unfortunately for that fellow.
Mihit An: What just happened? Why are you guys so morose? as

if we've been defeated or something!

Then Ray An and the princesses related the entire episode… well mostly the princesses, because Ray An was in no position to make sense of the conversation… he was busy looking for something to cover the body, basically to afford some respect to the fallen heroine. To him that was what the Drakaina was, a very brave one at that.

Esmella: "This is baby Tantara. How tiny and vulnerable he is, isn't he? Nothing like the monster that King Bhimsenna described." She said pointing to the tiny curled up hatchling. Virann, who till then was full of bitterness and vengeance, couldn't help kneeling down to stroke the shivering hatchling's head, in a tender gesture of assurance. "There, there," he said "you're safe with us little one, you're safe…" The baby's eyes turned to look into the face of his benefactor and almost instantly knew he was secure in kindness and love here forward. Dragon's have a sixth sense you know?

Ray An who was crushed to bits with this tragic encounter, could hardly get a few words together … he just stood there looking at the body of the Drakaina…he was miserable.

Amelika: Come on Ray An cheer up, at the least you should be happy that you have been able to save the future of our planet Doryu!!

Ray An: "How can I? I've just slain an innocent mother!" The big man with a soft heart also with the soul of a poet, he would most certainly pen his feeling before the night fell, just as he always did with every bump in the journey of life. And he did.

His eyes welled up as he looked around at the others, silence had descended. It was a strange sight indeed. They had just been so successful in actually saving the future of the planet, the biggest feat they had ever accomplished! Even defeating a band of battle-hardened dragons, yet there was no room in anyone's heart to savour the victory. A pall of gloom descended on the rest of the warriors.

And as they all stood around in silence, then it was decided to give the mother dragon a Doryuan farewell at the palace of Phillislot. This was the way of the Doryuans, it didn't matter which part of the planet you came from, if their actions caused the demise of anyone, they would provide a royal resting place for the deceased. The dragon's body would be wrapped up and taken by the warriors back to the castle, accompanied by Princess Esmella, Ray An, the warriors and baby Tantara. Amelika and Mihit An were heading back to the cave to inform Grandriks of the "good" news...

The Voice falls silent

Grandriks had time for a long and engaging conversation with the future king Bhimsenna. =He learnt a lot about the tactics employed against the dark forces, what worked and what didn't work …. He learnt how the king had grown up and what exactly were the circumstances of the all the royals by the time he came to the throne. All this he wanted to learn so that, history shouldn't repeat itself. But knowing how unpredictable life on the planet is, one could never be too certain of what the future held.

One thing the great sage knew for certain, no one would remember what happened by the time they reached back to the castle of Phillislot. He knew the mission would be successful, so he knew the law of the chronicle,

"If perchance you stumble upon a vision of the future…remember friend to savour then for… for time, a wisp of time …will erase the dream… and you be left amazed and wondering where that time had gone!"

All of a sudden there was no response from the King anymore, Grandriks could only hear the sound of water dripping somewhere deep inside the darkness … then a stream of bats flew out from above the rafters….

Grandriks continued to call into the dark "Hello! Hello! Your Highness are you still there? Your highness… answer me please…?"

But there was a cold silence … the cave echoed with the sound screeching bats…. then he knew all was well and time that old dreary keeper had gone back to ticking in right again.

Grandriks told the warriors who were with him: Maybe the Prince and Princesses have captured the baby dragon Tantara and the future King has reestablished his rightful reign over the kingdom….a quiet comfort engulfed him as he and the others turned and walked out into the sunshine…

No sooner had they emerged from the cave when Amelika and Mihit An arrived. Grandriks was happy to see them and hear of the rescue of the baby Tantara… they also told them the sad news about the baby's mother!

Grandriks: "Every being must be given an opportunity to turn a new leaf. It's sad she never got her chance, but then again, her son will become a truly good dragon once he learns the truth about the price his mother paid for his freedom"

Mihit An: "then there's this fellow! Gentlemen" (he addressed the warriors pointing at the chained dragon). By now the dragon, who heard the complete story, was reduced to a bundle of shivering nerves! "Take this whipper-snapper and banish him to the planet Eiben. But be sure to inform the centaur leadership before you do!"

"Yes Sir". Quipped the warrior.

By the time they returned to Phillislot, no one remembered the story or why they had brought back this hatchling. All they remembered was the battle and the defeat of the evil dragons. Somehow, they knew the Drakaina was the good mother of the hatchling. So, they could only report the matter the battle and the tragic death to the King of Pymra, Bhimashtra, The Queen Mother of the great Seas, General Uriah and the elders of the kingdom how the future of Doryu had been saved from being ruled by evil dragons.

Only Grandriks knew the secret of the future king Bhimsenna, because he existed outside the space time of Doryu.

On hearing the news of the success of the mission, a council of Doryu meeting was called. The Queen Mother of the great Seas made a formal recommendation to the council leaders "Ray An

the Giant, The Princess and Princesses have set an outstanding example of bravery, in the face of so much danger. I recommend that they be awarded the special medal for great achievement in peace time "The Honour of the Green Planet".
There was unanimous agreement with the recommendation. The quarter master of the king's guards was informed of the evening's investiture ceremony and chief of the palace kitchen was also informed of the feast that would follow.

So that evening after the mother of Baby Tantara was given a Royal Farewell, all five of the brave hearts were honoured by King of Pymra, the Queen Mother, and all the people of Doryu. With all the ceremonies behind them, the great feast commenced.

The king learns of the secret

As the night wore on Grandriks regaled the king and all those who had gathered there to celebrate this memorial occasion, about the exploits of the future King. All king Bhimsenna's troubles with the Evil Dragons and his series of defeats before the intervention of the current royal families and their warriors, not to mention the heroics of Ray An the Giant.

The King was proud that his grandson turned out to be a wise and brave king! But Grandriks had sworn him to secrecy, with a solemn oath, that he would never ever repeat a word to anyone... that he would take this awesome secret to his grave.

True to himself Ray An the giant had written a beautiful verse about the tragic end of Tantara's mother... but he just couldn't get himself to recite the poem. So, after dinner and before the bard began to play their music, Abby the Gail, friend of Princess Esmella read out a beautiful Poem he had written a while earlier.

It was an emotional poem and Ray An felt he could not read it without tears welling up in his eyes... so requested Abby to please read it on his behalf. He wanted to make a public confession of the mistake he made, so that his heart could be still and quiet again.

The moon hung low over the open lawns of the palace, the fireflies lit up the starry sky and as silence descended upon the waiting crowds, Abby stood up and walked to the front of the audience... and her gentle yet powerful voice carried the precious words across the silence of the night...

The Bleeding-Heart Mother

She didn't deserve what she got

T'was I, T'was I, I cried

who struck that mortal blow

The poor thing now rested there

her life just ebbing away!

Nothing like those evil ones,

Who fight to rule the planet

Her only care, the little young,

For whom she bled to die,

Please she said oh gracious sirs

Be so kind as to know

I was once a goodly soul much the same as you!

So please I plead take care of him

Teach him to grow up wise

My one wish, she said, for my precious son

My darling son to be raised up good and worthy

If you could do such a blessed thing

My life was not in vain…

Her pleading eyes turned to look once more at him

Had we known the purity

Of her simple heart

We would've held back that fatal blow

That snuffed out her precious life.

And now she'd be happy

And she'd be here.

But alas… The purest of heart

Go the soonest, it seems.

So, rest in peace, young mother dear,

Know that your son is safe and sound

For tonight he sleeps a peaceful sleep

Amidst true friends and loved ones!

The Language of the Doryuans

The Doryuan language is called the Uryanos. It does have earthly origins Legend has it that Uryanos is derived from the earliest earth language, spoken at the Tower of Babel, in what is now the country or Iraq. In those days all living creatures spoke one language, but they grew wicked in their effort to defeat the Triune.

So, they built a huge tower called the Tower of Babel in order to reach into heaven and capture the Triune. Needless to say, they were struck by a curse that made them suddenly speak in different languages! So, since they could not understand each other, each language group went their own way! One group eventually settled on the sister planet Doryu and brought the language of Uryanos with them.

The sages on Doryu teach the ancient at their places of higher learning, in order that everyone can understand each other. These linguists are highly respected members of the Sage community and have a special place among the planet's governing body. They teach that most of the words originate from a Norse dialect of earth.

Note: There is no word for goodbye.
On Doryu one never says goodbye to family, guests, visitors because they are always in your heart.

• Bethalaka	(Beth a laka)	Success be yours
• Curiodem	Cu rio dem	Kingdom
• Curio	Cu rio	King
• Comrio	Com rio	Queen
• Nflma	Niflima	Princess
• Tflma	Tifflima	Prince
• Hersir	Herr sir	Commander
• Herkloedi	Herk Lo di	Armour
• Dyer	Dier	Hooved Animal
• Reka	Re Ka	Avenge
• Kalfe	Kal fe	Cafe
• Sysla	Sys La	Business
• Bears	Bears	You
• Anlamon	An la mon	Get better
• Aama	A ama	I or me
• Bethabara	Beth a bara	Come again.
• Koya	Ko ya	Hello anytime of the day.
• Bullah	Bul lah	Welcome
• Degud du bears	De Gud du bears	Nice to meet you
• Aama bears a bara		I will see you again
• Aaman Nuite Philo		My name is Philo
• Aama lif undo mountain lake		I live by/ near the mountain lake
• Kua r bears boro?		Where are you going
• Kua hiv bears		Where have you come from
• Manumalo		Victory
• Bullah vid rodulong Doryu plutan		Welcome to the Sunny Doryu!
• Vandliga	Vand Liga	Carefully
• Bardagi	bar Da gi	Fight
• Halr	Ha Lar	Hero
• Risna	Ris na	Hospitality
• Sukha Sikuku		Happy Holidays
• Sukha Nyh Ar		Happy New Year

Famous quotes of the Ooryuans:

"Since one cannot escape the clutches of aging, it's better to die proudly fighting for something noble"

Dragon sayings :

There is nothing great about being better than others, true greatness is being better than your old self.

Warriors of the Kings Guards:

Choose your destiny, for a creature does not become a hero by birth right but by his or her actions.

Warriors of the Mounted Corp:

Stand and fight for to run you'll only die a tired defeated warrior.

Fairy sayings:

When fear rules your actions, you fall into error.

Royal Quote:

The House of The Great Seas. To remain alone is to snub the flames of greatness from spread.

White Wolf quote:

Where the Wolf's ears are, the teeth are near

Elf quote:

A creature is rich if he has Valour NOT gold.

Dragon quote:

Die with honour don't live with shame!

Mother's Union of Doryu:

Mistakes happen because life doesn't come with instructions

Royal quote of The House of Pymra:

Like the sword that is sharp in the sheath– so must the mind

and the spirit be in the body.

Could the legend of Doryu be a reality or just fiction?

We have carefully collated many elements from the young author's discussions that took place over a period of a year. The idea behind presenting a comprehensive overview of the history of Doryu and their inhabitants is to aid readers to garner a fuller understanding of the story and the significance of each event.

This book reflects on the so-called myths, legends and everyday facts. These are knitted together to form a complete picture of the life and times of Doryu. As the saying goes there is no smoke without fire, so there is no myth or legend without an iota of truth at the core. I say this because many a nation's myths and legends stem from some true happening somewhere in the mists at the dawn of time, very very long ago.

So even scripture could be the basis of some truth, who knows, truths that were lost to the sands of time.

Cdr Maddox Matter
Editor